**FICTION FROM
NORTHERN IRELAND & WALES**

First published in Great Britain in 2010 by
Young Writers, Remus House, Coltsfoot Drive,
Peterborough, PE2 9JX
Tel (01733) 890066 Fax (01733) 313524
Website: www.youngwriters.co.uk

Disclaimer
Young Writers has maintained every effort
to publish stories that will not cause offence.
Any stories, events or activities relating to individuals
should be read as fictional pieces and not construed
as real-life character portrayal.

Foreword

Since Young Writers was established in 1990, our aim has been to promote and encourage written creativity amongst children and young adults. By giving aspiring young authors the chance to be published, Young Writers effectively nurtures the creative talents of the next generation, allowing their confidence and writing ability to grow.

With our latest fun competition, *The Adventure Starts Here ...*, secondary school children nationwide were given the tricky challenge of writing a story with a beginning, middle and an end in just fifty words.

The diverse and imaginative range of entries made the selection process a difficult but enjoyable task with stories chosen on the basis of style, expression, flair and technical skill. A fascinating glimpse into the imaginations of the future, we hope you will agree that this entertaining collection is one that will amuse and inspire the whole family.

Contents

Nantyglo Comprehensive School, Nantyglo

Pontarddulais Comprehensive School, Pontarddulais

St John's on-the-Hill School, Chepstow

Ysgol Hendre Special School, Neath

The Mini Sagas

The Chase

The mouse ran and ran and tried to get back into his little house. *Just another mile to go,* he thought, whilst the cat was snapping his jaw and chasing him. Then the cat grabbed his tail and he went down in one, the satisfied cat went to sleep.

Daniel Cushing (13)

Untitled

Bobbie, a spaniel, woke up and couldn't find her toy. She looked for it everywhere, even under my bed. Bobbie was upset because she couldn't find her toy and went to bed. Bobbie's bed was lumpy. She looked under her bed and saw that her toy was there all along.

Katie Logan (10)

Hercules The Weak

Hercules was a god who thought himself strong enough to kill a mortal. Hercules went to Earth with his spear and shield. He went and found a mortal. *Bang! Bang!* The mortal won. Hercules was beaten. He returned all bloody and beaten. Unlucky chap, better luck next time!

Thomas Klee (11)
Barry Comprehensive School, Barry

Invasion

In Britain we made a rocket which went six weeks ago. We've had no contact with the rocket.
Five minutes later … The rocket crashes on Earth and six aliens come out and they disappear into the city!
We've found them and killed them and the city is safe.

Matthew Lovesey (11)
Barry Comprehensive School, Barry

The Hairy Beast

'Oh no!' he shouted. He was being chased by
a hairy revolting beast through his village …
Suddenly two beasts jumped out of nowhere. He
screamed, their jaws snapped, he shouted, 'Help!'
Villagers chased them into a corner and cornered
them. One hour later the zoo came.
Lions! He thought.

Lewis Jones (11)
Barry Comprehensive School, Barry

Red Anxious Nan

She stumbled, crept and hid. A dark figure entered. Anxiety took over. *Slam!* … Nan locked in a cupboard.

Another voice bellowed, 'Oh, what's occurin'?' It was Red Nessa, her grandaughter. A gun cocked and Nan leaped out of the cupboard. The figure … A wolf! His crew was howling, 'Dinner time!'

Samuel Broughton (11)

Barry Comprehensive School, Barry

The Wolf And The Seven Kids

In a dark wood lived a sly wolf. Nearby lived
Mother Goat and seven kids. Whilst she was
shopping, Wolf devoured the kids except for one
who hid inside the clock. Mother was devastated.
Meanwhile Wolf slept under a tree. She found
Wolf, cut him open and found her family.

Antonios Grigoriou (12)
Barry Comprehensive School, Barry

Beef With The Butcher

The butcher steadied his knife above the squealing cow. He raised the knife and *bang!* the cow was gone.

The following day the butcher raised his shutters; staring out, unsure what he was seeing. The view quickly became clearer - twenty-five angry cows, vengeance in their eyes. The butcher gulped.

Cameron Crow (12)

Barry Comprehensive School, Barry

The Battle

It was the biggest fight of his life, he paused, his weapon lay in front of him, his prisoner stood silently. He took a step back and shot. His prisoner fell as the bullet cracked against the bar. Half the stadium rose in joy as he dropped to his knees.

James Scott (12)

Barry Comprehensive School, Barry

Game Over

Guns roared, terrified people screamed, shots were being fired frequently. Men and women were getting killed everywhere. Then disaster struck as General Buckney finally fell down, soldiers couldn't do anything. He was dead. The young boy started crying. Then his mother said sympathetically, 'Don't worry, it's only a video game.'

Thomas Jones (12)

Barry Comprehensive School, Barry

Nessa The Riding Hood

'Oh what's occurring Gran? I'm coming over yours, OK?' Nessa set off … She was on her way and … a fat creature came. It was ugly, it had large teeth, hairy moles, lots of them! It was fat and hideous, disgusting. It scared the hell out of her. 'What's occurring Gran?'

Gabriel Cleary (12)
Barry Comprehensive School, Barry

Punishment

The trembling boy was thrown onto the cold
mats, surrounded by a merry audience. He
turned around and put his back to the beast. He
knelt down and prayed. He stood up, the beast
looked and stared in amazement as the boy rose.
The bell rang and the fight began.

Dominic Todd (13)
Barry Comprehensive School, Barry

The Deadly Fall

There she was on top of that long grey skyscraper. She had to clean every window of the building. She got the machine and got to work. She finished ten, then twenty, then she passed out. The machine broke and the door opened. She fell. Then a voice said, 'Fumble!'

Callum Sullivan (13)

Barry Comprehensive School, Barry

The Awesome Caterpillar And His Laser Gun

The awesome caterpillar was eating a leaf one day and then *pow!* a tiny zebra with twelve faces and eighteen feet started chewing his leaf. Now the caterpillar would not stand for that. So he got out his laser gun and zapped that zebra to Poland and back, *pow!*

Jac Limbrick (14)

Barry Comprehensive School, Barry

Joe And The Seven Midgets

Joe went out and decided to stroll to the shop.
On his journey, loud music blasted. He looked to
either side and saw disco lights. Party! He strutted
over and inside met seven midgets. After dancing
and having fun, Joe's drink got spiked. Shockingly,
by his stepdad, disguised as Jordan.

Ryan Fennell (14)
Barry Comprehensive School, Barry

15

Time Flies!
School Must Be Fun!

Every morning I wake up and get ready for school, but then by the time I turn around it is time to get up and get ready for school again. They say, 'Time flies when you're having fun!' Therefore school must be fun. Don't miss the opportunity to succeed well!

Daniel Taylor (13)
Barry Comprehensive School, Barry

The Awakeness

Lying lifeless, distraught, deflated, cowering in his own shelter of self pity. Gazing at his brother who just four minutes ago was fighting for his last breath. Plastered in blood, his eyes were still open, but there was nothing behind them. He began to wonder … *was it all worth it?*

Mason Lewis (13)

Barry Comprehensive School, Barry

17

The Tramp

Last night I was going to a party and a man came towards me and muttered, 'Do you have some change?'
I ran but I don't know why. Then I went to the doctors for a check-up. I walked inside, he checked me ... He said, 'You're dead!'

Jay Pitcock (14)
Barry Comprehensive School, Barry

The Three Little Dogs

There once lived three little dogs called Woofus,
Barkus and Sid; they had an evil uncle, Bruce.
One day Bruce went for a walk and munched on
the house of straw belonging to Woofus. He then
scoffed Barkus' house of twigs. Later he saw Sid's
house of bricks … and gorged.

George Douglas Cooper (12)
Barry Comprehensive School, Barry

Soaring

We set off skimming the beautiful blue sea, the speedboat full of anxious couples. After watching the first couple whose faces changed from horror to pure excitement, my dad and I were ready to paraglide.
Thumbs up and off we went. What a tremendous feeling, soaring into the sky!

Harry Lambert (12)

Barry Comprehensive School, Barry

The Life Of Meg The Cat

There I was, an ordinary moggy. I heard the uprights talking. Suddenly they chased me and threw me into a case! I cried but they didn't listen. Then they put me on a table a hundred feet high, then this giant man poked and prodded me. Then the needle came …

Sion Parry-Flavell (12)
Barry Comprehensive School, Barry

21

My Mini Saga!

I'm writing my mini saga, but I'm short of ideas. I want to make it funny by using onomatopoeia. It's hard because I've got writer's block. I just don't know what to say, I could rewrite Goldilocks or go swimming down the bay.
If I don't start now I won't …

Jack Broun (13)
Barry Comprehensive School, Barry

22

The Titanic 21st Century Style

It started in Liverpool. Everyone was excited about going on the unsinkable ship. The ship went to New York but before, let me tell you, they hit an iceberg. A giant dragon saved them, it took them back to Britain and everyone survived.

Joe Dearing (12)
Barry Comprehensive School, Barry

23

Untitled

Little Chav was going to her mates in the deep
woods. Halfway through, a bad gangster jumped
out and robbed her. She walked on, and the
gangster followed her. Not knowing he was still
following she got to her mate's.

'What's the matter?'

'Someone robbed me!'

'Is that him?'

'Yeah!'

Josh Campbell (12)

Barry Comprehensive School, Barry

Thumbnail, The Minotaur

Thumbnail chased the deadly wolves down
craggy coasts, away from his resting place. Then
he caught one and ferociously ate it; there were
four left. He drove them into a devilish trap. They
were surrounded by other minotaurs. The dead
wolves were covered in dirty, red and cold blood.

Cory Myers (11)
Blaengwawr Comprehensive School, Aberdare

25

Eagle

He swooped and dived, grabbing his prey with his big, sharp talons. He flew back up into the sky, landing on his nest, where he tore off the fur, as he bit into the mouse's white skin, ripping his flesh. After he'd finished he flew away to find another one.

Chloe Taylor (12)

Blaengwawr Comprehensive School, Aberdare

Tropical Island

The sun is beating down on my face; blue sky, the tropical breeze blows through the trees into my face. The waves gently ripple onto the warm, golden sand. Delicious fruits hang from the tall tropical tree. The seagulls nest in the cliffs and rivers flow peacefully into the ocean.

Ellys Panniers (12)
Blaengwawr Comprehensive School, Aberdare

Collision

Crash! The car came off the road and tumbled down the mountain. The man came flying through the windscreen and he nearly died. The man was lying on the floor with a missing arm because he'd hit a big rock. He was really hurt and not going to survive.

Lewys Nott (12)

Blaengwawr Comprehensive School, Aberdare

Nightmare On Halloween

I rang the doorbell, not realising the horror. Next,
the door flung open, I walked into the bloody
living room. I don't know why but I carried on
through the house until I entered one room. I saw
a man. He came towards me. I was dead …

Calla Davies
Blaengwawr Comprehensive School, Aberdare

29

The Meat Shop

He looked up at the man, his eyes as black as
coal. He said to me, 'Do you want this tasty meat?
The cold-blooded pig who was once running
around?'
I said, 'No!'
I ran out into town. Someone said, 'Are you OK?'
I said, 'No. Go away!'

Laura Phillips (12)
Blaengwawr Comprehensive School, Aberdare

The Holiday

It was banging on the roof. The rain was so heavy! We were on our way to Wales. By now my brother was shouting and crying. Finally we were there! My aunt's, so boring. But when we got there, she wasn't even there. All that for nothing.

Sophie Price (12)

Blaengwawr Comprehensive School, Aberdare

31

The Black Shadow

Alison looked round the corner, her face was as white as snow. She walked over to the deep black shadow, going closer and closer to it. She heard a sound. She turned round and hid. Then she went back over. She heard a 'miaow'. Aww, it was just a kitten.

Maryssa Jeins (12)

Blaengwawr Comprehensive School, Aberdare

The Raging Rhino

The sound of stomping came loud and clear,
then suddenly it appeared, smashing everything
in its way. The raging rhino caught sight of its
target. Its anger grew and then the strangest thing
happened. The rhino wasn't angry anymore, it
was friendly. But suddenly it charged … !

Luke Whitcombe (12)

Blaengwawr Comprehensive School, Aberdare

The Ghost In The Attic

I walked quietly up the stairs, there was no sound, only the faint ticking of the clock hanging on the wall. I reached the top and then *thump, thump.* I screamed. Silence! I heard *tap, tap.* I was in the attic. I carried on and climbed the ladder. I screamed!

Kelsey Love (12)

Blaengwawr Comprehensive School, Aberdare

Shark

He swerves and darts left to right, circling his prey. Then he launches out of the water. *Swoosh! Crunch!* He tears the person's pale white skin and eats the bloody flesh and bones. He buries his head under the blue water and searches for another terrified victim …

Rhian Picton (12)

Blaengwawr Comprehensive School, Aberdare

35

The Prisoners

'No! Jacob stole the ring!' John screamed. No one listened. He was locked away. Suddenly he could hear someone approach. The barred door opened. 'Come on, let's go,' the man whispered aggressively. John followed. Slowly the man pulled off his mask to reveal his angry bitter face. Jacob shot John.

Sophie Quinn (12)

Ffynone House School, Swansea

36

On The Shore

Crash!
Water flowed in as waves slammed against the
ship. Shouts of fright filled the air as a wave swept
through the wooden floor. The people were now
knee-deep in water. Hope was fading as the ship
sank under the water.
'Argh!' someone called. 'Thank goodness, we're
on the shore!'

Jemima Pope (12)
Ffynone House School, Swansea

The War Zone

There I was in the battlefield. I was camping thirty
feet from the bombsite with thirty terrorists
guarding it. We got out a riot shield - there were
ten remaining, they all met a bloody death. We
tried to disarm the bomb but it was all too late …

Harry Pope (12)
Ffynone House School, Swansea

The Split

Cheryl was packing her bags, shouting at Ashley,
telling him that he'd hurt her badly. 'As I said in
one of my songs, Ashley, you're a heartbreaker,'
she sang to him.
He replied, 'But we've got to fight for this love!'
Cheryl grabbed her things and walked out, crying.

Georgia Griffiths (12)
Ffynone House School, Swansea

Lion's Dinner!

Mouse said hello to Lion as they went out to
tea. 'What's for dinner?' asked Lion, 'For I have
company.'

'Roast rabbit, my good sir, with mouse on the
side!'

'Oh no!' cried Mouse. 'That's how my uncle died!
Bye-bye Lion!' shouted Mouse and quickly ran off
to hide.

Harriet Williams (13)

Ffynone House School, Swansea

40

The Joker

Carol ran into the room. 'We've been expecting you, Carol,' came a voice from nowhere. Then a figure swooped down and landed next to her, his face as white as a sheet of paper.
It was over in a split second and Carol lay on the floor, bleeding to death.

Elizabeth Silverberg (12)
Ffynone House School, Swansea

The Age Of Frandosaur

In the year 2010 a massive nuclear explosion happened in northern England that killed hundreds of people. Nobody knew that a small purple lizard had been affected by the nuclear contamination and it created the mighty Frandosaur. Related to Godzilla and standing over 400 feet tall, he marched towards London …

Alexander Sheldon (13)

Ffynone House School, Swansea

The Lego World

Did you know that there are more solar systems in the galaxy than ours? Yet there is only one other system that we know about that only has one planet. The planet is a world just like ours, but it's not dying. The planet is called the Planet of Lego!

Rhidian Hall (13)

Ffynone House School, Swansea

43

The Man Who Was Teased

A man was teased because he was quite large.
Let's just say he was told off when all the cake
was gone even when it wasn't his fault.
One day, he was so cross he decided to do
something about it. He went to the gym and got
fitter.

Rhodri Jones (12)
Ffynone House School, Swansea

The Fat Cat!

Once there was a cat who was very fat. One day
he fell into a well. After that, he ate a rat and saw
that he would never be slim again. In his sorrow,
he went to borrow a great slimming machine.
Now he is really slim and really trim!

Daniel Huxtable (13)

Ffynone House School, Swansea

Additional Surrender

We surrendered to them, one by one. We were
tied up and piled next to the building we had held.
They started pulling us until five were lined up in
a row. They were given a brief trial, then shot.
Then I was picked and the gun was on me …

Finn Nolan-Bennett (13)

Ffynone House School, Swansea

Aliens

Everyone was screaming and running away from the sinister shadow of the UFO. It hovered, releasing thousands of destroyers. Beams from the mother ship scanned the night, attacking combat planes with ease. Explosions created dark clouds of dust and debris.

'Cut!' the director shouted happily. 'Time for a coffee break!'

Tomoya Awata (14)
Ffynone House School, Swansea

47

The Unsolved Murder

She stared, too afraid to speak. Who had done this? Why to her? There were so many questions, yet no answers. It felt like the world stopped. Every heart stopped beating. She stood there unable to move a muscle. She was trapped and then a steady hand gripped her shoulder …

Elysia Gregg (13)

Ffynone House School, Swansea

The Perfect Holiday?

As Adam sat on the plane he came across a
Middle Eastern man who was uttering words
from another language. He wasn't a judgemental
person but he thought the man may be a
terrorist. Suddenly there was a huge explosion.
The last thing that Adam saw was his evil smile.

Jack Grey (14)
Ffynone House School, Swansea

Hunted

The deer pranced through the trees in the moonlit forest one cold winter's night. However she was being chased by something not entirely human. Out of the shadows the creature appeared, grabbing and pushing her to the ground, effortlessly holding her whilst it hungrily ripped out her soft tender throat.

Katie Watkins (13)
Ffynone House School, Swansea

Paranoid

Trembling, she glanced over her shoulder. She was sure he was there. She returned to her mirror, and was shocked to see him, corpse-like, gaping behind her. She whipped around but he had vanished. He was following her, she knew it. This thought was too much. Everything went black …

Freya Koutsoubelis (14)
Ffynone House School, Swansea

51

It

It crept around in the darkness looking for one person. It was unaware of what it would meet. Its hands and feet worked in unison, fighting its way around the complicated cotton maze it was stuck in. It started to get scared. Tears rolled down its sad, bewildered face.

'Babies!'

Benjamin Francis (13)

Ffynone House School, Swansea

My Dream

I watched the brave courageous paramedics save
many people's poor defenceless lives. That night
I had an inspirational dream; my dream was to be
just like those fearless paramedics.
Today I am the heroic one who is saving people's
lives. I am now living my dream and I love it!

Elliott Thomas (14)
Ffynone House School, Swansea

Bravo

The curtain unfolded to reveal an enchanting radiant figure, softly yielded in a flawless white gown. She moved gracefully, since a toddler it had always been her ambition. The orchestra stopped. She gingerly took a step centre stage and bowed. A deafening applause from the audience circled the theatre … Bravo!

Elizabeth Bater (15)

Ffynone House School, Swansea

A Betrayal

'I know Paul can't come but we can still see the film.' As I entered the cinema with my sister instead of my boyfriend, we squeezed quietly into the row. *Oh no!* I thought.
'Oh no!' I heard Paul say, as I looked at the hand he was holding.

Hannah Francis (15)
Ffynone House School, Swansea

55

The Model

Posing for her first modelling photo shoot Rosie started the set with a fantastically sweet figure taking pictures of herself. Long into the evening her moves, smiles and personality shone through. Ready to review her photos she suddenly became angry. Bewildered, Rosie realised that the lens cap was still on!

Angharad Hall (14)

Ffynone House School, Swansea

56

The Ballerina Betrayal

A group of terrified ballerinas huddled close, trembling. Stricken stage crew stood around her body. She lay lifeless in the bright dressing room light, bloody as her unopened red bouquet. The choreographer wept sadly - 'Someone call 999!' Despair filled the theatre.
Somewhere in the wings an understudy stood secretly grinning.

Rowann Gorvett (15)
Ffynone House School, Swansea

Scott And The Unfulfilled Dream

Scott was very talented at maths but his love was dancing. He always wanted to be a dancer but his parents made fun of him. He wanted to be in the 'Strictly Come Dancing' competition but because his family and friends were making fun of him his dreams were crushed.

Jacob Gregg (15)
Ffynone House School, Swansea

Hope

My ambition in life was to be an actor. A simple but hard goal to achieve. People don't realise the effort it takes. All I ever wanted to be was an actor. From a child I always looked up to the big Hollywood actors. But I guess dreams die eventually.

Simon Morgan (14)

Ffynone House School, Swansea

Climbing The Highest Mountain

He would get to the top, nothing could stop him,
no matter how many innocent people he hurt, it
didn't matter. He would get to the top. The end
was so close he could almost reach it. He reached
out, a little further, but suddenly he fell back
down again.

Sofia Grammenos (14)
Ffynone House School, Swansea

One Dream, One Goal, One Failure

They had lived and died, fought and failed. All for a dream, all for one man's twisted ambition. The Holocaust; a bloodstained mark on the ground of Germany. A thing to be remembered but never repeated. To go down in history, never to be forgotten. Millions lost because of Hitler.

Myles Dyer (15)
Ffynone House School, Swansea

When The Battle Is Won

He reached for his blade. Eyeing my own dagger,
I knew this was life or death. He was about to
die. He lunged. My body reacted instantly. He
landed hard on the ground, my dagger piercing
his stomach. The fear was still visible on his face.
It was finally over.

Demi Rodriguez (15)
Ffynone House School, Swansea

62

The Actress

I want to be an actress. I've tried many times for auditions in roles in programmes such as 'Coronation Street' and EastEnders'. However, I've never actually been able to star in any. My ambition is to get better at acting and be famous like Angelina Jolie. Well, I can dream.

Alice Bosworth (14)

Ffynone House School, Swansea

63

Sprint Finish

'You've been training your whole life for this moment. People worked themselves to death to pay for your coaching. Millions of people helped you to get where you are. Now go and make them proud!'
He gets ready for the 100m sprint, the gun sounds. *Bang!* He trips, he falls …

Jack Palmer (15)

Ffynone House School, Swansea

64

The Ruined Singer

Andy was a talented sportsman, he could play sports phenomenally. He was a sports prodigy, but Andy had a dream that one day he could be a singer. He couldn't fulfil this dream because his friends would always make fun of him. His dream would be ruined forever.

Peter Jones (14)
Ffynone House School, Swansea

Dark Ambition

'Murder is worth the power it gives you,' said Leo as he pulled the trigger. With that one action, he had given himself power over a million people, he had become what he always wanted. A leader. And all because his ambition had been able to overcome his quiet conscience.

David Eves (15)

Ffynone House School, Swansea

Revenge

1576AD, 12th April. Silvio sprinted from the burning farm building near San Gimengino. His entire family had been murdered by the mercenary or the fire, he didn't know. He had survived by hiding in the loft. He jumped out the window escaping the blaze. His family would be avenged …
Soon.

Thomas Warren (13)
Ffynone House School, Swansea

Who's There?

Tom heard a bang, late one night. He panicked, jumped out of his bed and bounded down the stairs. Blood racing, he saw a light from the cupboard under the stairs. He turned the handle of the door and found a poor girl crying. Tom was staring at a ghost.

Niamh Burns (15)

Garvagh High School, Garvagh

My Bike

I got on my bike and went for a cycle. The sun was shining, there was a nice breeze hitting me in the face. The birds were singing. The wind started to get stronger, it started to rain so I turned to cycle home. Then I fell off my bike …

Aaron McElwee (14)

Garvagh High School, Garvagh

69

My Horror

The frightening sound of the sharp blades got louder and louder as they came closer and closer towards me. The *snip, snip* made me anxious. The woman in white breathing down my neck. Fumes made me dizzy, spinning, spinning, *thump!* I fell off the chair at the dreaded hairdressers!

Louise McDonald (15)
Garvagh High School, Garvagh

Will It Ever Stop?

It got darker and darker, the screaming got louder
and louder. Screams of fear. As I peered around
the corner, I saw dark red evil eyes beside me.
Suddenly everything got faster, the screaming
stopped and then I saw light.
That was the end of my scary ghost train ride.

Andrea Collins (15)
Garvagh High School, Garvagh

Rude Awakening

One day I was walking along my lane, minding
my own business, when all of a sudden I got hit
over the head with something hard. I woke up in
hospital staring down a loaded gun … *Bang!*
I woke up in a cold sweat. It was just a bad
dream!

Deborah Scott (14)
Garvagh High School, Garvagh

My Big Dog Johnny

My big dog Johnny with teeth so big and strong
and sharp. They bite through bones like a knife
cutting through butter.
My dog started a fight. Johnny tore at the other
dog then the dog legged it. Big dog Johnny
showed him who was the boss!

Nathaniel McAllister (14)

Garvagh High School, Garvagh

The Happy Head

There once was a man who never said no.
Friends took all his possessions. Bandits took
his limbs and body so a happy head was all that
remained. The bandits decided to repay him with
a scrap of paper which said, 'Fool'.
The little head cried with delight, 'Thank you!'

Georgina Boyd (15)
Garvagh High School, Garvagh

Abducted

Up high in the atmosphere, the UFO flew. I'd
landed on a red-hot planet. I saw a little green
figure come out from behind a weird plant. He
said, 'Peace be with you, brother.'
I stared at him confused. In his eyes a reflection.
'Argh!'

Tara Wilson (13)
Kilkeel High School, Kilkeel

Brian's Mini Saga

'Once there was a princess who was kidnapped
and taken to a dark castle guarded by a dragon.
Three years she was kept there, but a knight
came and saved her. The end. By Brian Newell,
aged seven.'
'Aww no!' exclaimed Brian. 'My mini saga's only
thirty-two words long!'

James Johnston (13)
Kilkeel High School, Kilkeel

Lost

I was isolated, alone, unwanted. The silence was uneasy. Leaves covered the entire grounds creating a kaleidoscope of colours. Fresh air brushed against my face. Night was approaching, darkness was rolling in. Silhouette figures lingered among the outskirts. Suddenly footsteps lurked behind me. Thunderous, deafening growls ripped through the air …

Sophie McKee (13)
Kilkeel High School, Kilkeel

The Picnic Proposal

The sun was setting in the coral sky. Jack and Kate were standing by their picnic mat, which was placed on the golden sandy beach of Marbella. They nibbled on strawberries and sipped champagne. Showered with affection, Kate stared into his crystal-blue eyes and slowly dropped to one knee …

Georgia Monteith (13)

Kilkeel High School, Kilkeel

Seat Stealers!

We were first. As we shoved through the door,
we saw our prize. The back desks. They were
ours. They were behind us but weren't giving up.
'They're our seats!'
'Not anymore.'
'Sit down; stop shouting.'
They sat, glaring.
A note fluttered to our desk, addressed 'Seat
Stealers'. We giggled.

Rachel Newell (12)
Kilkeel High School, Kilkeel

79

Crystal Planet

I cautiously explored the unknown planet, feeling a burst of energy and excitement. The sandy surface glistened beneath my feet as I explored the great glass crystal landscape. Without warning a strange green creature appeared from behind one of the crystals. I stepped back, hoping it wouldn't get any closer.

Ryan McConnell (12)
Kilkeel High School, Kilkeel

The Dark Storm

Suddenly the weather started to change. Waves crashed angrily against the bottom of the cliff. The clouds began to cry, their tears of rain beating down to Earth; the trees shook side to side. In the distance a mysterious silhouette stood still as if it was glaring at me.

Emma Nicholson (13)

Kilkeel High School, Kilkeel

Lost!

I was lost … Lost in an open space. There were giant dragons swooping and soaring through the sky. They soared down before my tired eyes, doing acrobatics. One came crashing out of control … I ran … It was coming violently. Dead meat!
Turns out I was lost … In my own dream.

James Nicholson (12)
Kilkeel High School, Kilkeel

The Follower

Someone or something was watching me, and I knew it. The winding street seemed to last forever. I was starting to wonder if this scene would ever change. Panic was suffocating me. If this thing wanted to take me, why couldn't it just do it without torturing me first?

Lynsey Norris (13)
Kilkeel High School, Kilkeel

Death Was Calling

As the razor-sharp claws ripped through my
flesh, I knew death was expecting me. I had
finished screaming. I no longer had the energy
to continue. The blood still gushed out of my
infected wound. Pain was no longer striking me.
Death was now in sight, slowly creeping closer …

Lyndsey Watterson (13)
Kilkeel High School, Kilkeel

The West

The wild, dusty West is surrounded by mountains peering down on the free stunning horses. Running like the wind. Eagles soaring against the rising sun. suddenly a crash of lightning; a boom of thunder; a storm was approaching. A team of horses reared, bucked and bolted in fear.

Kirsten Patterson (12)

Kilkeel High School, Kilkeel

It ...

My feet pounded against the earth as I sped forward in the ice-cold rain. It was right behind me, getting closer to its target. Suddenly I was falling towards the earth, all I could taste was the disgusting soil. That was it, I was done for. It was over.

Emma Paulson (13)
Kilkeel High School, Kilkeel

Stuck

They stripped me, they violently shoved me, slamming the thick, heavy, monstrous door behind me. My heart pounded repetitively from the effort of trying to force myself out. Eventually I plunged towards the cold, hard, wooden floor. I just had to give up. I lay helplessly on the stiff floor.

Naomi Patterson (13)
Kilkeel High School, Kilkeel

The Photograph

The snow-covered mountains glistened in the sunlight under the clear blue sky, creating the perfect background. Beneath the mountains, thousands of green trees, topped in white. Alpine skiers making their way down the mountain. He sat down on the bench, pulled a blanket over him and said, 'I wish.'

Andrew McKee (14)
Kilkeel High School, Kilkeel

Halo

As we charged the elite stronghold we knew the day was ours. The cries of the fallen echoed in our ears as we gazed anxiously upon the daunting task which lay ahead of us. We charged, not knowing what to expect. Banshees fired upon us but eventually we conquered Hell.

Arnold McCullough (14)
Kilkeel High School, Kilkeel

Saw

In shock his eyes flew open. Room black, not knowing what to do. Suddenly a screen came on saying: 'I wanna play a game'. To survive, the person in the screen tells him to cut his eyes out to get a key for a device on his head. Will he … ?

Glen Thompson (14)

Kilkeel High School, Kilkeel

The Battle

The machine guns were chattering behind me. My enemy was charging towards us. Raindrops were hitting me on my head, like small stones falling from the sky. I saw my target lying on the worn-out, muddy ground. His bullet was hurtling towards me like a thundering asteroid …

Andrew Stevenson (14)

Kilkeel High School, Kilkeel

Fifty Feet High

Edward and Ella were on the mountains. As
they were walking along, a sudden gust of wind
came out of nowhere and blew Ella off the edge.
Edward tried to hold on but his weak, feeble
arms couldn't, so he let go. He tripped over and
fell off as well.

Carly Pulford (13)
Kilkeel High School, Kilkeel

The Dark Night

I went to bed thinking of the movie I had just watched. I slowly closed my eyes. Then I heard a loud bang. I woke up, ran down my stairs. I walked towards the window. There was lightning then a dark shadow appeared at the window … It was my dad.

Glenn Wright (13)

Kilkeel High School, Kilkeel

The Fall

He fell so fast. His eyes streaked and he started
screaming for he was flying so fast. Earth zoomed
closer at one hundred mph. His skin hurt from
stretching like a canvas … He hit water as the
crowd cheered. He was the first to jump off the
highest diving board!

David Goodwin (12)
Kilkeel High School, Kilkeel

The Riot!

I was sitting in Anfield one Saturday when a riot broke out. It only took ten minutes until I could smell and see the massive fire. The groundsmen and police were going mad. They went especially mad when some fans took this opportunity to break into Liverpool's gift shop.

Darryl Stewart (13)

Kilkeel High School, Kilkeel

The Shadow

It was a dark windy night. Two girls were walking home from a club. Suddenly they heard footsteps and drips from a pipe. They turned around, looked and saw a shadow. They walked on as the man came up behind them. He grabbed them and whispered, 'Gotcha now girls!'

Chloe Graham (13)
Kilkeel High School, Kilkeel

Untitled

The cold sun was shining through my window. The birds sang as I woke up but, I thought to myself, *D-Day has come!* I got dressed and ran outside to my turkeys. They were all in the corner, looking scared as I came in. *If only they knew,* I thought.

Matthew Skillen (13)

Kilkeel High School, Kilkeel

Football Madness

It was the last day of the cup and Ryan was determined he was going to score the winning goal. He ran towards the goal with speed, then out of nowhere he was taken down. The referee wanted to stop the game but he got up and won the cup.

Simon Wilson (14)

Kilkeel High School, Kilkeel

The Storm

Smashing through the waves the brave little boat pushed on. I could see the mini skipper at the helm, fighting against the current holding her steady. A tsunami was ready to break and all on board would perish …

'Ah Mum! Don't pull the plug out yet!'

Scott Cousins (14)

Kilkeel High School, Kilkeel

The Sweet Shop

Joey walked to the sweet shop. 'Darn!' he shouted. The sweet shop was closed! 'How am I supposed to get my sweets now? I'm just wasting my energy by just standing here! I guess I will just have to use the sweet shop next door to it!'

David Beck (12)

Kilkeel High School, Kilkeel

The Graveyard

In an old graveyard, two dead men jumped out of their graves. They started to squabble, fight and rip each other to shreds. They lost their arms and legs so they couldn't get back to their graves. To this day they shuffle around the graveyard at night.

Matthew Annett (12)

Kilkeel High School, Kilkeel

Rusted

As Chris entered the air-locked chamber he could see how withered and rusted the abandoned submarine was. Chris entered the control room and found a decomposing body on the floor. 'This really is a deathtrap.' Suddenly the metal started to dent. 'It's the pressure.' There was a crash. Then death.

Rhys Clements (12)
Kilkeel High School, Kilkeel

The Naughty Fox And The Three Hens

Three golden brown hens were sunbathing when
… *bang!* Someone was stealing their eggs! The
blaring sound of clucking was sonorous! The hens
all scurried into their house, chasing away the
mischievous fox. Putting up a fence was the best
solution to their problem. 'He shouldn't be back!'
cheered the hens!

Carol Graham (12)
Kilkeel High School, Kilkeel

The Three Plump Pigs

Three plump pigs lived in different time periods.
The first pig built a house of straw, it wasn't very
sturdy.
Three hundred years later, another pig built a
house made from sticks, but it could burn.
Another hundred years later, a pig built a house
from bricks, it was perfect.

Matthew Henderson (12)

Kilkeel High School, Kilkeel

The Three Smart Pigs

Three pigs left home and built their own houses out of wood, hay and bricks. A wolf came to pig one and two and blew their houses down. They went to pig three's brick house and boiled water. The wolf climbed onto the roof, fell down the chimney and died.

Danielle Brown (12)
Kilkeel High School, Kilkeel

The Ice Cream Man

Standing on the beach, terrified of the ice cream man. Sneaking down the beach, children went to see him … they were gone. The ice cream man reached him, he wasn't going to go up but he was too tempted. He went up … he was gone. Never to be seen again.

Anna Hill (12)

Kilkeel High School, Kilkeel

Power Of The Future

My name is Danny and I live in Palm Beach. I got these powers on a Saturday night. A green light shone on me. The next morning the green light did something to me. I had super strength and a super suit and weapons to defeat evil. Ha! Ha!

Ruairi McKee (13)

Kilkeel High School, Kilkeel

107

Yellowstone

Yellowstone, a catastrophic event just waiting
to happen and today was the day, the super
volcano detonated. It exploded with such force
the Earth's orbit was altered. A mushroom
cloud blocked out the sun and we were plunged
into darkness. The pyroclastic surge came.
Machiavellian gas crept into my nostrils …

Robert Barber (13)
Kilkeel High School, Kilkeel

Unexpected

Stars glistening in the frosty winter sky. Streetlights shimmering. Trees swaying back and forth. Deadly silence crept menacingly over the town. Something was going to happen. The cars came rallying past me. Another going the other way. The next thing they were on the road. Glass smashed. They were dead.

Emma Johnston (14)

Kilkeel High School, Kilkeel

Where Did Mum Go?

There we were. Just sitting in my room, waiting
for Mum to bring us out movie treats. Just then,
the light bulb blew and the room went silent!
I could no longer hear anything! My mum was
missing! Where had she gone? She had gone to
the shed!

Tiffany Edwards (14)
Kilkeel High School, Kilkeel

The Birthday Surprise

Out of the darkness a large black figure appeared.
He asked me if I was Anne. He said, 'Come with
me,' pulling at my arm. He took me to a hall and
the door swung open and after the screaming
was …
'Happy birthday Anne!'

Jennifer Gordon (14)
Kilkeel High School, Kilkeel

Trigger

Aaron shoved the revolver into my unwilling hands, aiming it at the seventeen-year-old I was supposed to shoot. His ungainly body was convulsing in terror and his baby-blue eyes begged for mercy. Dismally I pulled the trigger and watched ruefully as his fragile life drained away.

Rebecca Davidson (14)

Kilkeel High School, Kilkeel

Goodbye Mummy

The fight was over, the love was gone. Mummy was dying but why? The doctors said she would survive. On Mother's Day it happened. I went to her but Daddy said she had gone to Heaven. He held me. The only mummy I have is a picture.

Emma Beck (14)
Kilkeel High School, Kilkeel

The Broken Heartbeat

I slumped beside his bedside, tearful and fatigued.
The tubes were a maze I couldn't find my way
round. I watched his heartbeat rise. What was
happening? Doctors whispered. Anxiety filled me.
My stomach groaned. I stared as his heartbeat
regulated. I sighed. I could relax, for now anyway.

Carla Hamilton (14)
Kilkeel High School, Kilkeel

Lost!

Trees rustled in the howling wind. Completely
lost, looking around for help, I started to panic.
Falling, I twisted my ankle. As I screamed, I saw
a dark shadowy figure coming slowly into view. I
shrieked even more but I heard a familiar voice
calling me. It was my dad!

Rachel Hutchinson (13)

Kilkeel High School, Kilkeel

Homeless

Scary, horrifying, terrible. This was how I described the poor man sitting at the side of my street. When I walked past him, his voice was like an owl screeching in the night. He tried to speak, but I could see he was in pain. Suddenly unconsciousness crept over him …

Naomi Haugh (14)
Kilkeel High School, Kilkeel

Distracted

The shadowy figure came out of nowhere. I swerved. The other car just appeared. I frantically left my vehicle and ran for my life. As I ran I realised what I had done. The pain I'd caused. Where could I go from here? There was no way out of this.

Louisa Hanna (14)
Kilkeel High School, Kilkeel

Dragon

It roared, hissed and growled. Out of its huge jaws came a ball of fire. It showed me its blood-covered teeth and dangerous claws. With one flap of its wings it was off the ground and twirling into the sky. As the dust settled, I watched it fly away.

Shannon Paul (13)

Nantyglo Comprehensive School, Nantyglo

Futuretopia

Aneurin, Keely, Imogen and Khia walked into the big, swirly, bright circle. When they finally stepped out the circle, there was something there staring at them with its huge scary face.

'Where a-a-are we?' ten-year-old Aneurin stuttered.

'Futuretopia,' smiled the thing. 'This is the future.'

'What!' shouted Imogen.

Courtney Edmonds (12)
Nantyglo Comprehensive School, Nantyglo

The Old Man

The old man would not wait, he was always first but this was his undoing. On his wedding day he rushed to cross the road, but his wife called him back to cut the cake. He cut the cake then ran across the road and got run over!

Lukas Sweet (13)

Nantyglo Comprehensive School, Nantyglo

My First Fish

I couldn't believe it! Up and down, round and round. It was so strong. I reeled in. It went back down. Up it came, closer and closer. You could cut the tension with a bread knife. Finally here it came! It was the day I caught my first fish!

Josef Sullivan (14)

Pontarddulais Comprehensive School, Pontarddulais

121

My Holiday!

I walked down the steps and the sun shone
straight into my face. I could smell fresh air, hear
planes passing and see the sea. Collecting our
luggage, we went outside, staring at everything.
There were trees, hotels with clear blue pools
and the sun shone brightly. Ibiza was great!

Ashleigh Jones (13)
Pontarddulais Comprehensive School, Pontarddulais

A Sorry Tale

One sunny afternoon, a brother and sister felt thirsty. They strolled up the hill. Once they reached the top, the young boy collapsed and plummeted down the hill, sustaining serious brain injuries. In her anxiety, Jill fell and went rolling down after Jack!

Olivia James (14)

Pontarddulais Comprehensive School, Pontarddulais

A Day In The ...

I walk through the intimidating door as white as a ghost. I make my way down the claustrophobic corridor. I sit in the corner away from all the adults. My mum sits next to me. She says it's going to be OK ... I hate the dentist! Oh no! My go!

Gafyn Donald (14)

Pontarddulais Comprehensive School, Pontarddulais

My English Lesson

I was sitting in English when suddenly army
commandos ran through the door. 'Come with
us,' they said. We rushed out of the class and in
the awaiting helicopter were my parents.
'Is everything alright?' I asked.
'Yes darling we just thought this was quicker to
get to the dentist!'

Ella Grey (13)
Pontarddulais Comprehensive School, Pontarddulais

The Big Bang

The roof starts to rattle, the house shakes.
Ornaments are falling. The dog is barking. A big
bang from downstairs. I start to walk downstairs,
shaking, petrified. I peek into the lounge and
'Argh!' A big red monster. It lets out a roar.
'Ho! Ho! Ho! Merry Christmas!' and vanishes!

Josh Ashby (12)
Pontarddulais Comprehensive School, Pontarddulais

The Glass Of Milk!

It's the wild west, bullets flying everywhere, one bullet just skims past a shooter. Finally a laugh is let out, a man behind the bar comes up and says, 'I only wanted a glass of milk!'

Joshua Barlow (12)

Pontarddulais Comprehensive School, Pontarddulais

Empty

I arrived home. The house was empty. I'm sure they said that they would be back by now. I explored the house. I wandered into the kitchen and sitting there was the ugliest beast I had ever seen. *That is disgusting* I thought to myself. 'Oh hello Auntie Louise!'

Rachel Phillips (13)

Pontarddulais Comprehensive School, Pontarddulais

The Mermaid

At the bottom of the ocean lived a beautiful mermaid, she had blonde hair and blue eyes. All of the mermaids were jealous, but they were kind to her. She said, 'Do you want to be like me?'
'Yes!'
So she said, 'From ugly to nice.' Then they were beautiful!

Jemma Nolan (11)
St John's on-the-Hill School, Chepstow

Who Am I?

Who am I? All I knew was that I was a
shopkeeper's daughter, at a young age I never
knew my mother, I would ask Dad but he would
change the subject. Yesterday I found an article
about Mum, no wonder Dad would change the
subject, she was a criminal!

Bethan Mulley (12)
St John's on-the-Hill School, Chepstow

The Break In

As I walked along the dark and gloomy road in the dead of night, there was a sudden urge in me to break into the house by me. I smashed the window open and jumped in … only to find that it was my own house!

Kane Johnsey (13)
St John's on-the-Hill School, Chepstow

131

Stalker

The man behind me was getting closer. I wished I'd never gone down this dark alley now. Why was he wearing that long black coat? What was he trying to hide? Then suddenly he put his hand on my shoulder and said, 'Sir, is this your wallet?'

Max Parry (13)

St John's on-the-Hill School, Chepstow

Dead Silence

It came and thrust its neck forwards. Its teeth embedded in my arm. My arm shook and I fell to the ground and it snaked away into the bushes. I was left for dead, no one around. I lost my breath and darkness cloaked me.

Emlyn James (13)
St John's on-the-Hill School, Chepstow

2012

Fear struck me as we flew over the cities that were sinking into the water from the massive earthquakes. But as we landed, Yellowstone had erupted and was heading for us, it looked like a huge cloud of fire coming towards us, but wait, we couldn't do anything …

Alex Gregory (13)
St John's on-the-Hill School, Chepstow

Snatch

My torch shone, trying to find the beast. The moon beamed on my gun. I heard a rustle. I saw it and its beautiful eyes glaring. I snuck closer, trying not to make a sound from the leaves. Tension building then *drip, drip,* dripping over me. I looked up …

Josh Reid (11)

St John's on-the-Hill School, Chepstow

Nursery

He held my hand, I didn't know what to do. I couldn't hear myself think. There were noises surrounding me, like a thumping in my head. My heart was pounding, I didn't know what to say to the man, but that's the thing, I can't talk.

Rebecca Cann (12)

St John's on-the-Hill School, Chepstow

Danger At 100°c

The fire was rapidly moving up the building, I had to get out. The room temperature was rising to the extreme, my life flashed before my eyes. I ran out the building, the bomb went off …

Guy Nicholas (12)

St John's on-the-Hill School, Chepstow

137

The Mysterious String

There it was, it was a string, but what would happen if I pulled it, would I die, or would something frightening happen to me? As I slowly moved my hand to pull the string, I was shaking with fear, then I pulled it and then the light came on.

Emma Smith (11)

St John's on-the-Hill School, Chepstow

Human Fear

There it is, the screams of horror, the nauseating
smell of terrified sweat. Ladies clasping their
mouths in desperation, not able to do anything.
The air thick with human fear. Hearing the sound
of your heartbeat, thundering like a drum. Your
worst nightmare. Your first day at primary school.

Annabel Ricketts (11)
St John's on-the-Hill School, Chepstow

139

Scream

I slowly turned my head and gazed at the screaming man lying on the floor, blood pouring from his chest. I looked up and saw a figure running into the distance. Suddenly a man with a camera came to the screaming person and said, 'OK take five is over!'

Nia Harper (11)

St John's on-the-Hill School, Chepstow

The Trick Of The Mind

He plummets down on the bitter, icy floor, skidding with shards of snow down the everlasting valley. Broken skis scattered over the helpless mount. Silence, here comes an apparition, a grizzly bear. Is this the appalling, horrific, gruesome, shocking end for him?

Cullen Middleton (11)

St John's on-the-Hill School, Chepstow

141

The Match

'Are you ready Steamy?'
'I've never been more ready,' Steamy nervously
replied.
Due to injuries within the squad, Steamy, an
87-year-old, was Wales' only hope in the World
Cup final against New Zealand.
With one minute remaining, Steamy burst
through the defence and scored to win the
match!

Billy Colthart (12)
St John's on-the-Hill School, Chepstow

Dead Man

It was a cold summer's day and the cars of the
city were rushing by, but one person was asleep.
Asleep for good. Over the noises of the city you
could hear the sirens the best. Suddenly two cops
entered just in time to see an unidentified person
running away …

Ben Mädler (12)
St John's on-the-Hill School, Chepstow

New Moon

Will I ever get there in time? I run through the red-clothed Italians. I see him alive, it's true. He slowly unbuttons his shirt to show his diamond skin. I run across the square's fountain. He hugs me back. I kiss him, our lips meet passionately. I love him.

Zahra Iqbal (13)
St John's on-the-Hill School, Chepstow

Haunted Scare

I opened the door and saw a man. He was tall and strong, I could tell that at a glance. Then he turned and I screamed. He had a scarred face, a sword dripping blood everywhere and fingers with claws like a cats. He took off the mask …
'Happy Halloween!'

Eleanor Hill (11)
St John's on-the-Hill School, Chepstow

Becoming A Dentist!

The clock ticked. Everyone was silent. All Adrian could hear was the occasional scream, and the odd cough. 'Not me,' he murmured. Another scream. The door opened, out emerged a tearful, bloody kid. 'Oh no!' said Adrian.
'Adrian Poet please,' said the dentist, while swirling his syringe into the air …

Joshua Peters (11)

St John's on-the-Hill School, Chepstow

Flames

I could not believe it, it was a real fire, I was trapped in the building and was like a sitting duck. I looked out the window and saw my trampoline. It was simple. I launched myself out of the flames and into the night air and onto the trampoline …

Edward Harries (12)
St John's on-the-Hill School, Chepstow

147

Worst Date Ever

My feet pounded on the mossy forest floor. His taunting laughter embracing me as if a lover. His soft footfalls behind me. Closer and closer he gets. I collapse, the ground swallowing me. *Bang!* The laughter stops. My head turns.

'Scream!'

I do. My last thought, *worst date ever!*

Natacha Dowds (12)

St John's on-the-Hill School, Chepstow

Tortured With Words

I sat on the seat shivering and scared. She opened the drawer and took out a giant stapler. She was going to torture me and strap me up. She stared into my eyes, hypnotising me. She opened her mouth, torturing me with words. 'Which earrings would you like?'

Victoria Willis (12)

St John's on-the-Hill School, Chepstow

149

The Predator's Hunt Down

The jungle was strangely silent and the tiger appeared lurking for food, sniffing and rummaging, hungry for his next meal. Something moved, he smelt it, the meat of a gazelle was close. He watched, he waited, he pounced. The startled gazelle had no clue. He was the tiger's lunchtime treat.

Zara Ward (11)

St John's on-the-Hill School, Chepstow

The Desert Island

One sunny afternoon Jim and Jake were rowing peacefully along the ocean's surface. Something big hit! *Bang! Crash!* They fell suddenly out of the boat and landed in the water. Sharks surrounded them. A yacht passed and they leapt on and it took them to shore.

Declan McGee (10)

St John's on-the-Hill School, Chepstow

151

Diving!

The diver before me dived into the ice water and did not emerge for an hour. It was my turn to dive into the wavy water. Under the waves it was calm and clear. As I swam, the waves clattered over my head. Then I slowly and carefully emerged.

Helena Davies (11)

St John's on-the-Hill School, Chepstow

I Shot Hitler

As I peered over the bank with a gun in my hand, I saw Adolf Hitler himself. I aimed my gun and someone saw me, I shot and got him right in the chest. But at that very minute I got a bullet in the back. I had been shot …

George Bettley (10)
St John's on-the-Hill School, Chepstow

The Alien And Me

The slimy green alien slithered forward, I was trapped. I panicked, cowering into the corner. I frantically looked around, nobody was in sight. Suddenly the alien duplicated itself twice and became three. I tried to run but there was nowhere. They captured me, but I saw a little white door …

Sarah Dobbie (11)

St John's on-the-Hill School, Chepstow

Seal Attack And Revenge

Swerving, cutting through the depths, danger of death everywhere. Racing and being chased by a grey blur. Dan gets eaten by Cannibal Craney and Ed gets bitten by Evil Emma. What should the fishes do? The fishes gang up on Emma and Craney. Both drown and the fishes are saved!

Daniel Taylor (11)

St John's on-the-Hill School, Chepstow

Speedy

The dog gathered speed as it hurtled down the road. The ear-splitting bark echoed off the houses. The boy was rooted to the spot, frozen with fear. The dog pounced, drooling hungrily. It soared through the air, floored the boy and gave him a huge lick.

Ellie Brasher (11)

St John's on-the-Hill School, Chepstow

Goal!

The ball smashes against the net. Shall I stay or
shall I go to Newcastle? Then sadness strikes me
with a flick of an eye, my dad's dead.
I'm on the bench. Biggest match of the season.
I come on, smash the ball into the net. I'm the
hero!

George Lewis (12)
St John's on-the-Hill School, Chepstow

Timber

As I crept through the dark, gloomy forest, my ears were stunned as a big crash came down above me. I lifted my head. I saw a tree falling from above me, I heard someone shouting but my legs were stuck to the ground. *Crash!*

Costner Lane

St John's on-the-Hill School, Chepstow

Quick

My heart was racing like never before. Quick, little bodies rushed past me. I couldn't feel my feet, legs … or anything.
This was the moment I'd been waiting for, as people stopped and gave up I could see the finish line … I'd won!

Gabrielle Antrum (11)
St John's on-the-Hill School, Chepstow

Untitled

I walked into the woods one day and I heard
screaming and gunfire. There before me stood
a man covered in blood. With a sharp look, he
pulled out his gun, aimed, *bang!*
I opened my eyes and saw a dead pigeon.
'Well do you want a go?'

Jordan Roderick (12)
St John's on-the-Hill School, Chepstow

I'm Scared!

I'm scared, terrified, don't let me do this. Let me
go, I've been waiting for this all my life. What do
I do? I'm having second thoughts. Do I let it slip
or give it a try? I'm scared, confused, annoyed,
feeling regret. What am I going to do next?

Elliott Spear

St John's on-the-Hill School, Chepstow

Kidnapped By The Farmer!

Running, screaming, he grabs her. She struggles but fails. He's too strong. He crams her in the back of the van. The door shuts. She's alone. Unsure where she's going. Heart pounding. *Screech!* The van stops. Sun beams. She emerges surrounded by mudstained pigs. She's home. No longer kidnapped.

Alishia-Maria O'Connor Shaw (13)

St John's on-the-Hill School, Chepstow

162

The Mysterious Unicorn

As the stars lit up the dark sky, I got up from the moist, fresh, cold grass and made my way to my house. Suddenly I got hit. I opened my eyes and saw that there was a white, shining, bold unicorn standing there watching me.

Efthimia Mastrogiannopoulou
St John's on-the-Hill School, Chepstow

163

Son

I'm the son of Poseidon, a demigod. Once I was fighting a Cyclops. It kept hurling boulders at me. Only my friend Tyren (another friendly Cyclops) could stop it. We had to trick it into the sea then run it over with a ship. It made a loud crunching sound.

Matthew Green (10)
St John's on-the-Hill School, Chepstow

Victorian Mystery

I poked my head round the top of the coffin of the pale old man who had wrinkles all over his face. The wind blew across the room. With my heart pounding I looked over again. The man was gone! Worried and scared, I shouted, 'Alive! He's alive!'

Billy Gill (10)
St John's on-the-Hill School, Chepstow

The Dangerous Waters

Jamie was on a cruise around the world.
Everything was peaceful until they entered the
Bermuda Triangle. The clouds turned black, the
waves crashed, lightning struck the boat, there
was a flash and Jamie disappeared. They never
found him, he was in another universe …

Jamie Winters (11)
Ysgol Hendre Special School, Neath

The Castle

One day a dinosaur saw a dragon. The dragon blew fire as he ran towards the dinosaur. The dinosaur ran into the castle. They roared at the guards. The guards jumped into cannons and slayed the dragon. The guards and the dinosaur celebrated. The dinosaur said, 'Cheers.'

Julian Probert (12)
Ysgol Hendre Special School, Neath

Friday's Adventure

On Friday I was playing on my Wii. Next thing I
knew I was helping Mario, Luigi and Yoshi fight
the Goombas at Koopa's castle. A battle took
place in Bowzer's throne room and we beat
Bowzer.
Suddenly I was eating my dinner with my family.
What a day!

Jonty Bodger (11)
Ysgol Hendre Special School, Neath

Command And Conqueror

In 2047 a storm shot to ground. It caused a
Tiberium field. GDL and Nod were fighting for
the third Tiberium war. The alien Serin created a
fight. Nod annihilated every blue zone. GDI was
inside Temple Prime. Nod and Serin died. GDI
won the third Tiberium war.

Adam John (16)
Ysgol Hendre Special School, Neath

Graveyard

One day a boy climbed the fence of a graveyard. He heard a voice. He went back in the night and saw a vampire. The next morning he heard there was a murder. He told his family and the police what he saw. They told him, 'Never go there again!'

Jamie Isaac (12)

Ysgol Hendre Special School, Neath

A Terrible Halloween

Once, there was a boy and girl. They were scared every Halloween. Their names were Jack and Helen. Their mother was called Alice. Every Halloween Jack and Helen were scared because a big scary monster came towards them. But it was a dream while they were sleeping.

David Evans (13)
Ysgol Hendre Special School, Neath

171

Kidnapped

A boy got kidnapped by an old man. He got the boy to do stuff that he didn't want to do. One day the boy stole a car and then he robbed the bank but he got caught by the police. The boy and the man went to jail.

Phillip Walters (12)

Ysgol Hendre Special School, Neath

The Biker War

There was a war between two bikers. Their names were Dwaine and Johnny. They'd got five gang members each. Dwaine's team were called 'Red Storm' and Johnny's team were called 'Biker Storm'. They began to start to kill each other and the Biker Storm won the battle.

Ashley Thomas (12)
Ysgol Hendre Special School, Neath

The House On The Hill

Once there were three kids: Mel, Jon and Jess
and they went to a big house. The house was
on a high hill and Mel, Jon and Jess went for a
sleepover. Things started happening and Jon went
to a room, someone killed him. Then they ran out
screaming!

Aimee Morgan (12)
Ysgol Hendre Special School, Neath

The Great Metal Dragon

One day a man made a dragon out of metal. One day the dragon came to life. It burned the town to the ground and it escaped to the land of dragons. The other dragons didn't like the dragon that was made of metal. He was sad.

Gareth Hopkins (13)
Ysgol Hendre Special School, Neath

Stacey And Gavin

Stacey met Gavin and married him. They were really happy together. Gavin then died, Stacey was sad, but was happy soon after. She disappeared for a while, the family became suspicious. Did Stacey kill Gavin or did he die of natural causes? I'll let you decide who killed Gavin!

Emily Williams (15)
Ysgol Hendre Special School, Neath

The Big Bang

The big bang was all he could remember. When he came round he told the doctor, 'Jimmy is my name.' Jimmy changed behind a curtain. When the doctor came back from the ward Jimmy was walking out the hospital door. A blue beam took Jimmy away …

Luke Gerrard (14)
Ysgol Hendre Special School, Neath

The Adventures Of Robin Hood

Robin Hood lived in Sherwood Forest, they made houses and dens. They had a fight against Prince John for King Richard and his soldiers. Robin Hood took from the rich to give to the poor. Robin met Maid Marian and they went on the horse to the castle.

Ashley Williams (11)
Ysgol Hendre Special School, Neath

The Adventures Of Robin Hood

Robin Hood went to Sherwood Forest with his
men. Robin fought together with Little John,
Robin Hood and Maid Marian lived happily ever
after!

Kimberley Hopkins (12)

Ysgol Hendre Special School, Neath

MW2

I was playing MW2. I hit a button and I was in the game. The helicopter was shooting at me, but I dodged the bullets, then came a big drop. There was a big jump but I made it, then I was back in the real world!

Jay Davies (14)
Ysgol Hendre Special School, Neath

Meeting My Friends

Dressed in my best clothes I head into town
meeting my friends on the dirty bus. We go round
the shops and buy our faggots and peas, great!
Bored now, back on the bus, still dirty! Home and
tired, shower and bed. Oh a lovely sleep!

Emma Thomas (14)
Ysgol Hendre Special School, Neath

181

The End Of The World

It's the near future. Mankind's in danger. A new threat! Dark depths. Creatures threaten Mankind. They are losing against the locusts. They still fight for their homes. Mankind decides to kill all of them, but their plan means they must destroy their homes. Mankind dies destroying the locusts.

Richard Williams (14)
Ysgol Hendre Special School, Neath

Aidan Davies Concert

Just before 8.00, waiting for him. People
screaming! Aidan came out and started dancing.
Went over, had a photo with him. Went home.
Lonely bus. Had a meal. Saw poster for next
concert. *Happy days!*

Zoe Davies (13)
Ysgol Hendre Special School, Neath

183

Once Upon A Time

Once upon a time there lived a boy and girl, Jack
and Jane. Jane went to live with a kind professor.
She visited a magic room and it went through to
a forest in the snow. A lamb was lost. Jane found
the lamb. She woke in the magic room.

Victoria Reed (12)

Ysgol Hendre Special School, Neath

Information

We hope you have enjoyed reading this book - and that you will continue to enjoy it in the coming years.

If you like reading and writing, drop us a line or give us a call and we'll send you a free information pack. Alternatively visit our website at **www.youngwriters.co.uk**

Write to:

Young Writers Information,
Remus House,
Coltsfoot Drive,
Peterborough,
PE2 9JX

Tel: (01733) 890066
Email: youngwriters@forwardpress.co.uk